To Ian Hamilton Gordon, K.P.
To Mum, and in memory of Tess the dog, J.L.

First American Edition 1993 by Kane/Miller Book Publishers
Brooklyn, New York & La Jolla, California

Originally published in England in 1992 by The Bodley Head Children's Books
an imprint of The Random Century Group Ltd., London

Text copyright © Jonathan Long 1992
Illustrations copyright © Korky Paul 1992

Printed in Singapore
1 2 3 4 5 6 7 8 9 10

Library of Congress Cataloging-in-Publication Data

Long, Jonathan.
     The dog that dug / Jonathan Long and Korky Paul.
          p.   cm.
     Summary: Relates, in rhymed text and illustrations, the
misadventures of a dog who can't quite remember where he has buried
his bone.
     ISBN 0-916291-44-8 :
     [1. Dogs—Fiction.   2. Stories in rhyme.]   I. Paul, Korky.
II. Title.
PZ8.3.L848Do   1993
[E]—dc20   92-15093
                                                              CIP
                                                              AC

The DOG THAT DUG

Jonathan Long and Korky Paul

A CRANKY NELL BOOK

KM Kane/Miller Book Publishers

Brooklyn, New York & La Jolla, California

There once was a dog who was a bit of a clot.
He'd buried his bone and forgotten the spot.

He sniffed round the garden in search of his nibble,
Till he sniffed something nice and started to dribble.

'That must be my bone,' he said, 'down in the muck.
I knew I would find it with a bit of good luck.'

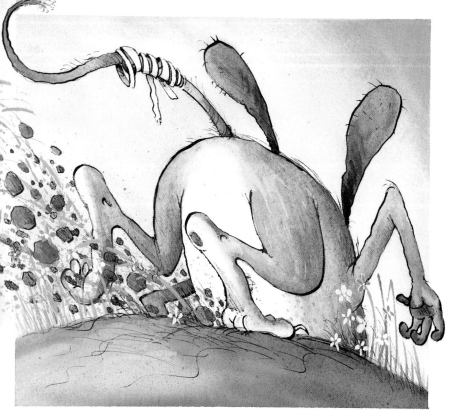

So he stuck in his paws and he scratched and he dug,
Till he found something hard and he gave it a tug.

But when he opened his eyes, guess what he'd found
– it wasn't the bone that he'd left underground –

It was an old brown shoe with a hole in the toe
That someone had dropped a long time ago.

'I can't eat that,' said the dog with a frown,
'My bone must be deeper, I'll dig further down.'

So he stuck in his paws, and he scratched and he dug,
Till he found something else and he gave it a tug.

But when he opened his eyes, guess what he'd found
– it wasn't the bone that he'd left underground –

But a coal-mining miner, all covered in soot,
Very surprised to be tugged by the foot.

'Sorry,' said the dog, 'I do beg your pardon,
I didn't expect to find you in the garden!'

The miner yelled 'Bad boy' and made quite a fuss
Then strode down the road to look for a bus.

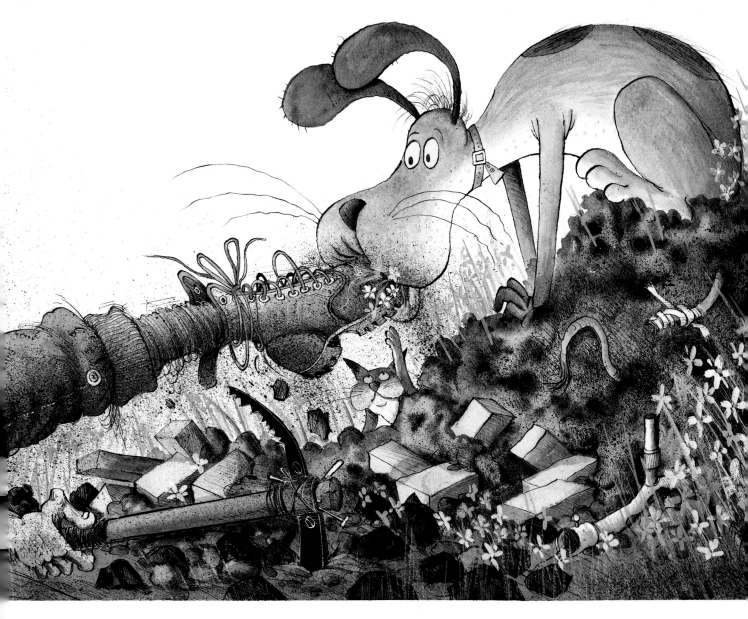

'Well I can't eat him,' said the dog with a frown,
'My bone must be deeper, I'll dig further down.'

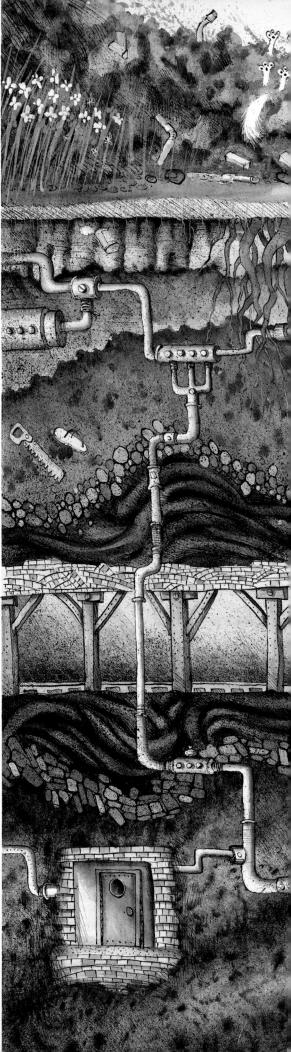

So he stuck in his paws, and he scratched and he dug,
Till he found something else and he gave it a tug.

It was terribly heavy and the dog had to battle,
But at last it came out with a shake and a rattle.

Can you guess what it was, the thing that he found?
A tubular train that chuffed underground!

With twenty-four carriages all full of faces
And a little fat driver taking them places.

'What are you doing? This isn't my station!'
Shouted the driver with great indignation.

'Sorry,' said the dog, 'I do beg your pardon,
I didn't expect to find you in the garden!'

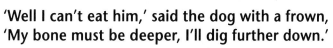
'Well I can't eat him,' said the dog with a frown,
'My bone must be deeper, I'll dig further down.'

So he stuck in his paws and he scratched and he dug,
Till he found something else and he gave it a tug.

But tugging it out was a terrible strain –
More of a strain than the tubular train.

And when it was out, guess what he'd found,
Buried away deep under the ground –

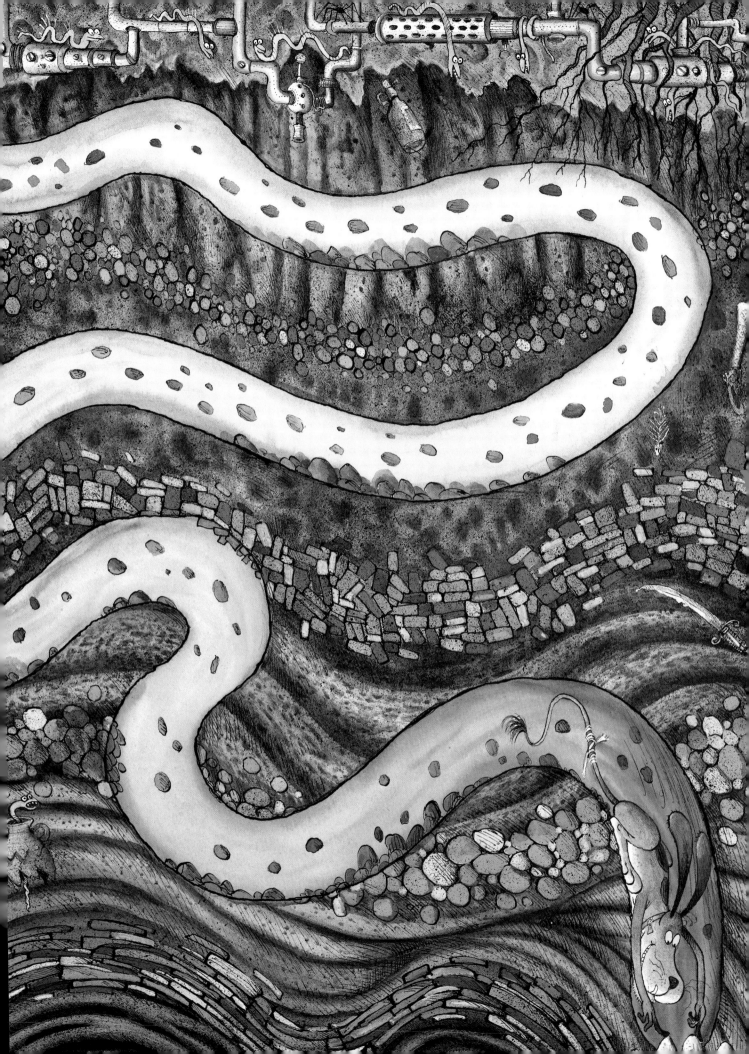

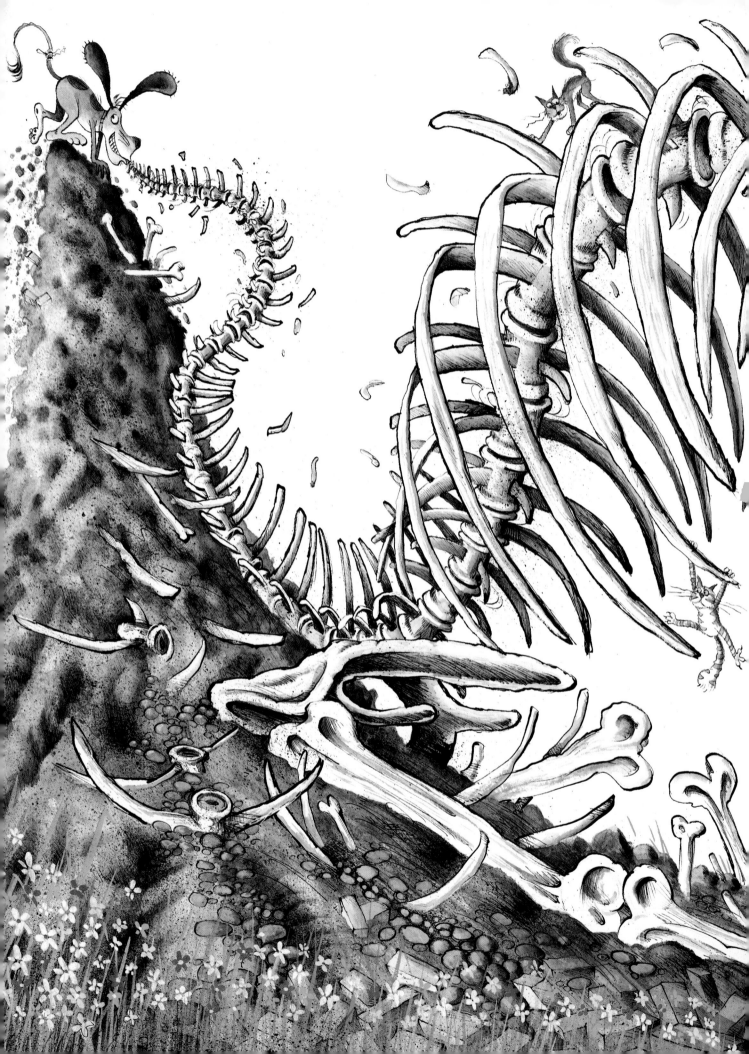

It was a bone at last, but it wasn't a single.
It was joined to some others and they all made a jingle.

There were big bones a-plenty and small ones galore
– all that was left of an old dinosaur.

'What a surprise,' said the dog with a smile,
'This pile of snacks will last quite a while.'

'Wait just one minute,' came a voice from aloft,
'Those bones are rare and not to be scoffed.'

A smiling professor was over his shoulder
With little round glasses and a shabby red folder.

'I'm hungry,' said the dog, 'those bones are my dinner.
If I don't eat them soon, I'll end up much thinner.'

'Look here,' said the prof, 'I'm not being funny,
Give me those bones and I'll give you some money.'

'Great!' said the dog, holding out one of his paws,
'Two million in cash and the bones will be yours!'

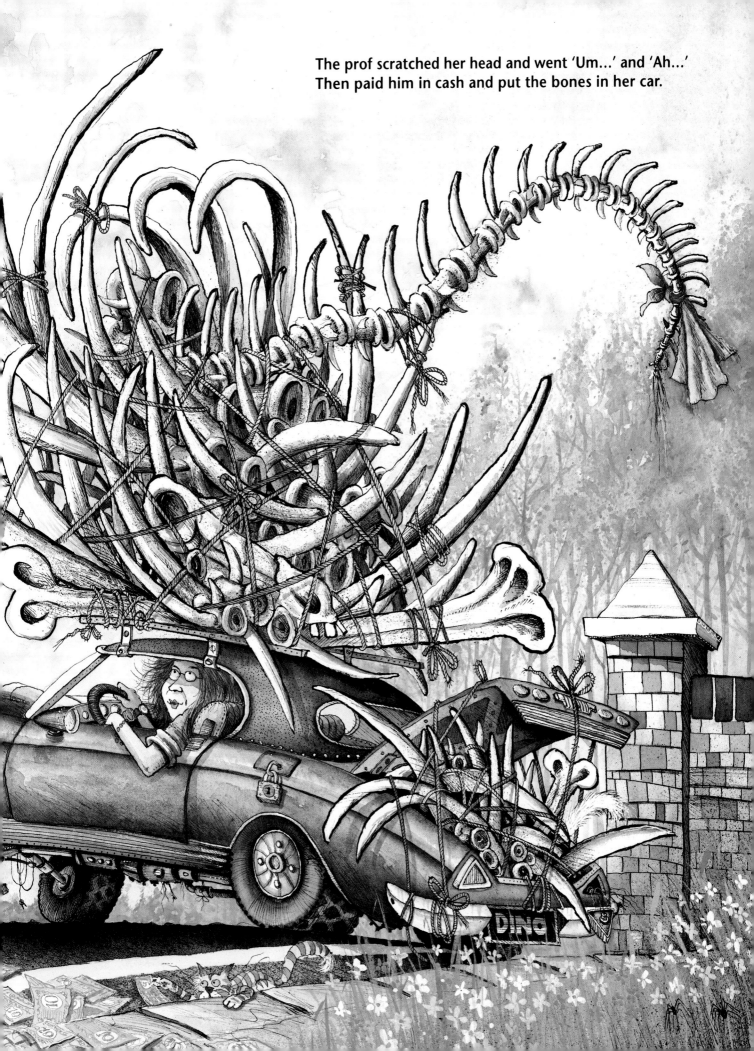

The prof scratched her head and went 'Um...' and 'Ah...'
Then paid him in cash and put the bones in her car.

When she had gone, the dog went to the shops
And bought a pound of his favourite chops.

And steaks and burgers and sausages in strings
And hot spicy pies, and other nice things.

Then he invited his friends for a beautiful dinner,
Where no one had bones – and no one got thinner.